D1540521

POLICE OFFICER BLAZE!

Adapted by Mary Tillworth

Based on the teleplay "Officer Blaze" by Veronica Pickett

Illustrated by Dave Aikins

A Random House PICTUREBACK® Book
Random House 🏛 New York

© 2019 Viacom International Inc. All rights reserved. Published in the United States by Random House Children's Books, a division of Penguin Random House LLC, 1745 Broadway, New York, NY 10019, and in Canada by Penguin Random House Canada Limited, Toronto. Pictureback, Random House, and the Random House colophon are registered trademarks of Penguin Random House LLC. Nickelodeon, Nick Jr., Blaze and the Monster Machines, and all related titles, logos, and characters are trademarks of Viacom International Inc.
rhcbooks.com
ISBN 978-1-9848-4940-3
T#: 642304
Printed in the United States of America
10 9 8 7 6 5 4 3 2 1

One morning, Blaze and AJ were at a railroad crossing, waiting for a train to pass. Just as the caboose was going by, it broke loose and rolled toward the river. It was full of chickens!

"Hang on, chickens!" shouted Blaze.

Blaze leapt in front of the caboose and dug in his wheels. But the caboose kept moving!

"It's too heavy. I can't stop it by myself!" he cried.

A police car roared up next to Blaze. "Officer Anna reporting for duty!" she said.

Officer Anna and Blaze stopped the caboose just before it reached the water.

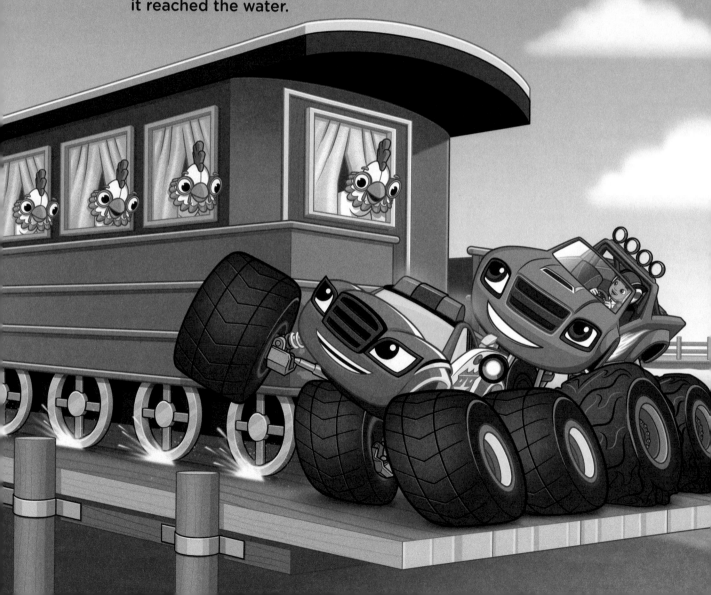

After they returned the caboose safely to the tracks, Officer Anna told Blaze and AJ that they were good at helping. "You should be police officers!" she said.

"I can handle that!" said Blaze. He transformed into a mighty police car with flashing lights, a siren, a searchlight, and an officer's badge. "I'm Police Officer Blaze!"

Just then, Officer Anna got a call to return to headquarters. "Blaze and AJ, I need you two to keep the city safe while I'm gone," she said.

"You can count on us!" Blaze declared.

As Officer Anna drove away, AJ checked the police emergency map. There were three emergencies in the city!

Blaze and AJ drove to the first emergency. They saw three little lost trucks that were trying to find their grandmas' houses.

"We'll use deduction to find them!" said Blaze.

"Yeah! Deduction is using the facts you know to get closer to an answer," AJ explained.

"What do you know about where your grandma lives?" Blaze asked each of the trucks.

"My grandma lives in a yellow building," said the first lost truck.
"My grandma's house has purple flowers," said the second lost truck.

"And my grandma's house has one window," said the third lost truck.

Blaze and AJ studied the houses on the street. By using the facts they were given, they found all three grandmas!

AJ checked the police map for the second emergency.
He directed Blaze to Clive's bakery, where they found the
worried baker out on the street.

"I made a cake for a big birthday party. But the party's far
away and I can't get there. It's about to start!" Clive moaned.

"Don't worry. We'll get the cake to the party on time!"
said Blaze.

As Blaze and AJ zoomed to the
party with the cake, they came
upon a huge traffic jam!

"We'll never get there with all these trucks in the way," groaned AJ.
Blaze had an idea. He switched on his flashing lights and loud siren.
When the other trucks heard the lights and siren, they made way
for Blaze and AJ to get through.

Blaze and AJ raced through the crowd. They were
almost to the party—but the door was closing!
"Time to use Blazing Speed," declared AJ.
Blaze revved his engine. "Let's *blaaaze*!"

Blaze and AJ flew underneath the closing door just in time!
"It's my birthday cake!" cheered Bump Bumperman. "And thanks
to you police officers, I can now have a very special birthday!"

After dropping off the birthday cake, Blaze and AJ went to the park for the third emergency. They found their friend Debris calling for his lost puppy, Pierre.

"We'll find your puppy," promised AJ.

Suddenly, sirens filled the air as Officer Anna vroomed into view. She had come to help!

"We'd better look around for clues," she said.

While Officers Blaze and Anna searched the park, they heard a tiny noise.
Arf! Arf! Arf!
Debris gasped. "I'd know that bark anywhere! It's Pierre! But where could he be?"
Officer Anna pointed past a large hill. "It sounded like it came from over there."
"Let's ride!" shouted Blaze.

Blaze, AJ, and Officer Anna drove over the hill to look for Pierre.
Blaze switched on his searchlight. "There's a trail of leaves
coming from that leaf pile."

"You're right, Officer Blaze!" said Officer Anna. "Pierre must
have gone through it."

"Follow those leaves!" shouted AJ.

The officers tracked the leaves to a mud puddle.

"Pierre must have gone through the mud puddle next." AJ shined the searchlight past the puddle. "See? Muddy puppy tracks!"

"C'mon!" cried Blaze.

Blaze, AJ, and Officer Anna followed the muddy tracks to a dog park.
It was filled with barking puppies!
 "Pierre must be one of these dogs," said Officer Anna.
 "But how are we gonna figure out which dog is Pierre?" asked AJ.

"We'll use deduction!" said Blaze.

"What facts do we know about Pierre?" asked Officer Anna.

"We know that Pierre went through a pile of leaves. So the dog we're looking for is going to have leaves on him," said AJ.

"Pierre must be one of these five dogs," said Officer Anna, pointing to all the leaf-covered dogs. "What other facts do we know?"

"We know that after the leaves, Pierre went through a mud puddle. The dog we're looking for is going to have muddy tires!" said AJ.

Out of all the leaf-covered dogs, there were three with muddy tires.
"I just wish we knew one more fact about Pierre," sighed Officer Anna.
"Wait! I remember something," said Blaze. "His bark!"
"Oh, yeah!" exclaimed AJ. He took out his tablet and played a recording of Pierre's bark.

"Which dog has the same bark?" asked Officer Anna.
Blaze pointed to the small black-and-white puppy. "That one!"
As Debris drove up to the park, Pierre barked happily and ran
to his owner.

AJ held up the police emergency map. "Check it out! Now that we've found Pierre, we've solved every big case in town!"

"Let's hear it for Officer Blaze and Officer AJ—the heroes of Axle City!" cheered Officer Anna.